Ian Hickman (actually his two middle names) is one of the pennames used by the author, a professional electronics engineer with more than fifty years' experience. With a BSc Hons, MIEE, MIEEE, he is a chartered engineer and a sometime member of various national and international standards committees concerned with equipment, systems level applications of electronics and communications. He is the author of over two dozen books (twelve titles, counting second and later editions) and over 300 magazine articles concerned with electronics.

This is Ian Hickman's first venture into fiction. His book *My Friend Farringdon* was instigated by a dream, completely forgotten, of which only the phrase "Spanking cat" remained. This prompted the present work which seemed to write itself, as ideas for the story flowed in abundance. The tale is told by Yellow Laughing S. Catt and covers his life and that of his friend, Farringdon Spanking Catt.

MY FRIEND FARRINGDON

A Feline Fantasy

IAN HICKMAN

AUSTIN MACAULEY PUBLISHERS™

LONDON · CAMBRIDGE · NEW YORK · SHARJAH

A CIP catalogue record for this title is available from the British Library.

ISBN 9781528928205 (Paperback)
ISBN 9781528965378 (ePub e-book)

www.austinmacauley.com

First Published (2021)
Austin Macauley Publishers Ltd
25 Canada Square
Canary Wharf
London
E14 5LQ

To my wife, Dot, for patience whilst books are in progress.

Note to Parents

This is not a large print book but this should normally present no problem. If a child complains that the words seem to wander around on the page, a visit to an optician is recommended. If prism correction is prescribed, it will usually provide a complete solution.

preface

This book recounts the story of two cats, Yellow Laughing S. Catt and Farringdon Spanking Catt, covering their first meeting and their various adventures. It is a book for children who like reading. All intelligent children like reading, so if you like reading you're obviously an intelligent child. So, read on and enjoy this unusual story. If you come across a word you don't know yet, just ask one of your parents-parents know everything. If neither of them is around, just look it up on the internet.

– Ian Hickman

Chapter 1
Yellow Laughing S. Catt

Hello; let me introduce myself. I'm a happy naughty cat and I live in a lovely home, looked after by Missus, a lovely lady who spoils me something rotten. She likes me to sit on her lap, especially in winter, and I can twine her around my little claw. She gives me nice meaty food or crunchy biscuity food, and there is always a bowl of fresh water there. If I'm good she'll put down a saucer with some milk in it and sometimes, if I'm very good, she will give me my all-time favourite, a boiled 'fish head'. The man of the house—I don't know his name so I call him MisterMissus or MM for short—he complains about the smell so I only get it if he is away, 'on business', as Missus calls it. If the house still smells of boiled fish heads when he gets back, I have to watch out or MM will aim a kick at me, so I always make myself scarce at such times. So, on the whole, I know that I'm a really very lucky cat, living in a big house, warm in winter, with red roof tiles and a big garden surrounded by a tall fence. I even have my very own tree in the garden, to climb.

Of course, the big people are very different from us cats. They know their father, whereas with us of course, any family history one learns from one's mother just comes to an end with us. It's left to my four sisters to pass it on to their daughters; my four brothers can't carry it on any more than I can. Anyway, I last saw my eight siblings just after being weaned; young Tommy came and collected me and took me to his home. Tommy is Missus's young son and we instantly became great friends. But I was in for a bit of a shock when I got there, as there was already a cat in residence. When I arrived, he growled at me in a very unfriendly way, so I named him Big Black Grumpy Catt, though the big people called him Lawrence. A few weeks after I arrived, early one morning before any of the big people were up, I found him lying on his side under the dining room table, motionless. When I approached, he gave no response, even when I poked him. Just then, Tommy came down and dashed back upstairs again shouting, "Lawrence is dead!" Of course, I had never seen a dead cat before—I suppose I shall die eventually; quite a sobering thought, really. I can't help thinking that they took me into the family because they knew Lawrence wouldn't be around much longer. I've heard it said that even the big people die eventually, though they seem to go on almost forever.

But getting back to my favourite topic, 'me', I'm generally known as Yellow Laughing S. Catt on account of my bright shiny fur and my cheerful disposition. Anyway, that's what all the other cats in the neighbourhood call me but of course, it's not my real name. Like every kitten, my real name was given to me by mother and I never reveal it to anyone–or at least only to a very good friend. By and large we are a jolly lot who all get on well together, except for the ginger tom who lives at number 27 and who sometimes barges his way into my garden. He is always trying to throw his weight about and bully one of us, if he finds us alone, but there are always several of us around so he is usually out of luck. We've noticed lately, though, that he is a bit lame and can't chase us anymore, after all he is very old now (in cat terms)–as much as 17 years, would you believe that? In fact, he can no longer get into my garden, unless he finds the gate open, because of the high fence all the way round.

Oh, and there's William Choco Brown Catt, he is really bright and an excellent mouser. In fact, I learnt a lot from him; actually, the only really bright ones among our group are just William Choco Brown Catt, and of course me.

Missus was always telling me not to go outside the garden, and for my first few months with them, I didn't. But I found that from my tree I could hop across to the top of the fence and now that my legs have grown stronger, I can just jump straight up there from the ground; even though my legs are rather shorter than usual, although the last bit does involve rather a scrabble with my claws. So, I have been to the 'outside' but always feel a bit embarrassed and remorseful when curled up on Missus's lap, knowing that she doesn't know that I have been over the fence.

Chapter 2
The Forest

My first outing beyond the garden was an adventure that might have proved my last. It was all so new and interesting and I was just sniffing around without a care in the world. I should have known better for suddenly a nasty big, brown long-haired dog sprang at me. Fortunately, he barked, which gave me just enough warning to make a dash for the fence and back to the safety of the garden. After that, I didn't venture out again for several days.

That was all years ago—it seems strange to think that now I have lived with Missus and Tommy for over two years and I feel I'm a fully grown up cat now. For much of that time, I have been exploring amongst the trees that lie just beyond the grassy field the other side of the fence, and have actually climbed most of them; all different shapes and sizes. Recently, I ventured much further into what the big people call 'the wood' and was lucky to find my way back again. The next day I ventured even further and after climbing a few trees, chased a few birds. One of these days I really will catch one. As I was there, I realised that I was hopelessly lost. I sat down and mewed ever so loudly, hoping someone would hear me and come to my rescue but there was no response. I took what I thought was the right way for home, but realised that I was more lost than ever. Thinking I might never see my nice warm home with its red tiles again, I sat down and howled like a kitten, I'm embarrassed to confess. After what seemed ages, a voice said,

"Hello...hello, what's this?"

I jumped with surprise and, turning around, found myself face to face with a big black cat with white paws. "I'm lost!"

"Well, are you now? Where do you live?"

"In the big house with red tiles and a high fence round the garden."

"And what are you doing here?"

"I just love exploring the wood. I've been doing so for years." To my surprise, he bristled and said,

"This is not a wood, it's a forest and it's my forest, although some people say it's called Underton's Wood."

"Gosh, do you really own all this?"

"Well, not actually own it, you know, but everyone who comes here knows that I sort of own it and that they can only come here if they ask my permission, which is what you ought to have done!"

He looked very stern, but not in a frightening sort of way so I said, "I'm sorry, I didn't know."

"Well, I suppose you want me to show you the way home. I'm afraid it's a long way."

"Oh yes, if you would, please." You see I was well brought up and taught to say please and thank you.

"All right, but before we set off, are you hungry?"

"Er, yes...very, actually."

"Oh, well I would have invited you to my home for a bite to eat first, young...er what's your name?"

"Yellow Laughing S. Catt!"

"I can see the yellow bit, but you're not laughing now, I guess. Well, while we're doing the introductions, I'm Farringdon Spanking Catt, but I'm afraid I've nothing at home suitable for a very hungry cat. So you'll just have to stay hungry till you get home. Follow me!" and with that, he set off at a great pace and I soon had a job to keep up. After what seemed like ages, the trees started to thin out and I could see the grassy field in the distance.

"I'm sure you can find your way from here now, young fella-me-lad Yellow Laughing S. Catt. Nice to have met you; you must come and see me again soon." I didn't like his jocular familiarity, but he was clearly older than me and obviously a wise old cat of the world, unlike the silly jolly young cats I play with in my garden. Then he added, "By the way, what does the S. stand for?"

"Well, it's er...too complicated to explain now. Anyway, how do you come to have such a funny name as Farringdon Spanking Catt?"

"Good point."

By the time I reached the fence and the safety of the garden, it was quite dark. Missus scolded me most severely for staying out so late but MM said "I thought, with luck, we might have lost him for good." Missus scolded him for being so horrible and Tommy actually kicked him!

My lovely home with its red-tiled roof

I meet Farringdon
Spanking cat in
Underton's wood

17

Chapter 3
Farringdon's Home

One weekday I set out early, even before MM had left
for work, and made my way across the grassy field
and into the forest, following the by now familiar
path to Farringdon's home. In case I'd forgotten
to tell you, I must explain that his 'house' is quite
different from the red tiled house in which I am lucky
to live. It is in fact, the hollow bole of a huge oak
tree, and is really surprisingly roomy inside, cool in
summer and nice and snug in winter.

"Hello, nice to see you. Nice to see you so bright and
early. I've only just finished my breakfast."

"What are we going to do today?"

"Well, I thought I would show you how a wise old feral cat lives."

He showed me how he caught wood mice, his favourite item of meat and also how, when that wasn't available one day, he could make do with various types of insects or nuts or berries or even an earthworm or two.

"Why don't you live in a nice comfy house like I do?"

"I used to, as a kitten, together with a nice lady and her two children Jack and Jill. Then one day a huge thing the big people call a pantechnicon-sort of enormous box on wheels-arrived and some strange big men loaded all the furniture, beds cupboards and things on board and drove away. Of course, I kept well out of the way while all this was going on, and afterwards the house seemed very quiet. I went in through the cat flap and found every room completely empty. Strange, I thought, how are they going to live without any furniture-not even a table or chair. But in fact, I never saw them again.

I went on living in the house for a few weeks, a month or more in fact; then one day a different pantechnicon arrived and unloaded a whole lot of furniture and that evening a different family of people moved in. They shouted at me and chased me out, every time I appeared, even in the garden. I already knew my way around the forest, so I moved in here, after chasing a squirrel away. Since then, I've done a bit of decoration and a few minor alterations and now I'm much more comfortable here than I ever was living in a house."

Farringdon sees his home emptied and never sees Jack and Jill again

21

Chapter 4
A Little Adventure

At least, that's what I call it now, compared with our really big adventure, but that came a lot later. That morning, I had wandered over, early, to Farringdon's place. He was just finishing his breakfast and said,

"Hello, what do you want?"

"What are we going to do today?"

"You're always asking that."

"Yes, but you live here in the forest and know it like the back of your paw."

"Right, err, I'll tell you what, we'll visit the pond. It's really huge—the big people call it the lake."

We set off in a different direction from usual and before long I was hopelessly lost; Farringdon kept pressing on until we came to a particularly dense clump of trees.

"This is a bit of real forest for you, remains of

Underton's Wood. I heard from a vagrant old feral cat–he never stayed in one place for more than a few days–that it once belonged to the Earls of Underton, but when the last one died, the old Countess, it 'passed to the crown'–whatever that means." When we came out the other side, there it was, a huge sheet of water that seemed to stretch as far as the eye could see.

We frolicked around for a bit and I even got a paw wet, something no respectable cat likes and I wasn't happy until I had licked it dry. After that we had the bright idea of walking right around the lake, at least, after we'd had a snack or two which we scrounged among the bushes. But we never did get right round because at one point we came to where a road passed by near the edge. Things were whizzing along in both directions; I never know whether they're called cars or motors, I can't tell the difference.

After we'd had a rest and amused ourselves watching the things whizzing by, we realised that evening was drawing in. By now there were very few cars and in a bit none at all. Then a car drew up near the water and a big fellow got out, holding a small cat in each hand. He walked up to the edge of the water and with his right arm, threw the cat far out into the water and the same with his left arm; only this one didn't go nearly as far. He then got back into the car and drove off into the dusk.

Without a word, Farringdon jumped into the water and started swimming out to the furthest cat, which was thrashing around, mewing forlornly. I can't swim, indeed I had never seriously set foot into water up to that point, but I couldn't just stand by, so I gingerly started to wade out to the nearer cat. As the water got deeper, I walked on my hind legs and instinctively paddled with my front paws. Soon I found I could grasp the young cat in my mouth, by the scruff of his neck. Turning back to the shore, I was so relieved when the water was so shallow that I could now walk on all fours again, and a moment later I was on dry land with a very frightened small tabby cat. It seemed ages, after shaking myself and licking the poor young cat dry, when an exhausted Farringdon waded ashore, dragging the other victim of that evil attempt to get rid of them. To my surprise, after a quick shake Farringdon was pretty well dry and in no time, he had licked the other victim dry too.

"What shall we do now—it's nearly dark?"

"Wait there with our two young friends," and with that, Farringdon disappeared. After what seemed like an age, he reappeared.

"Follow me!" he said peremptorily and led us to a narrow deep dell surrounded by tree trunks and bushes; down there we didn't feel the chill wind which had sprung up. We found a few berries and settled down to sleep, all huddled up together in a heap, to keep warm. Next morning, I said,

"Now what?"

"You must have a brainwave."

"Sorry, I don't do brainwaves."

"Well you're a lot of good, aren't you?" But then it happened! I had heard on my way through the garden to meet Farringdon, the previous morning, that Ginger Tom from number twenty-nine had died in the night. Was this the answer?

"I know a house where they have just lost their cat, run over, I heard. There will be lots of cat food there going to waste…"

"That's more than a brainwave, it's an inspiration, come on."

It was nearly mid-day by the time we got to number 29 and all squeezed through the paling fence into the back garden. Farringdon told the two young cats—that he had named Jack and Jill after the two children he knew before becoming feral—to go and stand at the back door, scratch it and mew loudly, while we hid out of sight. After what seemed like ages, we were afraid they might just give up, the back door opened and they were invited in with 'Oohs' and 'Aahs'.

"That's another problem solved then, thanks to you." I glowed with pride at this praise and thought to myself, there, I really am as clever as William Choco Brown Catt. On the way back to Farringdon's place I said,

"I didn't know you could swim and how come you got out almost dry?"

"It's not something I'd ever do for pleasure; I can't even remember the last time I was in water. But my mum told me that my dad was a Turkish Van Cat, which is why my fur is half as long again as yours, and it's very water repellent."

Chapter 5
A Death in the Family

It happened like this. It was about a year after our little adventure that one day Missus forgot to feed me. But fortunately, Tommy knew what to do, so I was alright. Unfortunately, Missus wasn't. She lay on the sofa, then took to her bed and soon after that they called a big white car thing, they called an ambulance and she was taken to a sort of big house called a hospital. MM went to see her twice a day and a couple of days later told Tommy to be brave, as Missus wasn't ever going to come home again. Then there was a big long shiny box in the front room and Missus was fast asleep inside it. Relatives came and looked at her and from my viewpoint half way down the stairs I could see her through the open door. She looked very pale and it didn't look as though she was breathing. Then some men fixed a lid onto the box and they took it away with Missus still inside it, in a long black car with big windows. Tommy was very upset and so was I and even MM seemed very quiet and upset too; not at all like his usual busy noisy self.

We all gradually got used to the situation when one day six months later, MM brought a lady to the house. They spent a long time chatting in the front room and then MM showed her around the house—I kept well out of the way. Her visits became more and more frequent, until MM told Tommy that he was going to have a new mummy. Two weeks later, there was something called a wedding and she and MM went away for a fortnight, leaving just me and Tommy living together—which I thought was great. I had just never got on with MM. After MM came back, she

I saw Missus in a long box,

for the very last time

moved in and I called her New missus, though I noticed Tommy did not look very happy about it. The very next day she complained that cat fur made her ill; 'allergic' she called it, and told MM that I would have to go. MM and I never got on very well together and despite Tommy's arguments, I think MM was glad of an excuse to get rid of me. I took the hint and left the house, forever. The night was cold and it was starting to rain, so I headed out of the garden, across the grassy field, into the forest and straight for Farringdon's home. It was quite dark when I arrived and I was wet, but I snuggled down next to him; he asked no questions at the time and in the morning, I explained the situation. "Oh dear, well of course you're welcome to stay here for a day or two, until you've sorted out somewhere to live, but you can't stay here forever; there just isn't enough food around for two feral cats in this forest."

Well, back in the garden I met Tommy who cuddled me and told me not to worry, as everything would work out all right. I didn't see how, but the next day he told me that Nobby Longtail Catt who lived with Grandad Jenkins at number 39, the house next door but one, had been run over the previous night and was stone dead. I knew just what that meant; like Lawrence, only there hadn't been a mark on poor old Lawrence, he just died of old age. But Nobby was in such a state that there was obviously no point in taking him to a cat doctor and Dominic, the grandson of Mister Jenkins, hurried with him into their back garden and buried him. Later, there was a big stone with writing on it, to mark the spot.

The family that lived at 39 were ever so upset, of course, but Tommy had a word with Dominic, and I was welcomed into the house to live there—well not entirely, at first. They carried me into the lounge and set me down in the middle of the carpet and I found myself face to face with a huge dog. It growled threateningly and advanced a little but I stood my ground, hissed as loudly as I could and stared it out. Eventually, it looked down and backed away and after that I had no trouble from it; in fact, we gradually became good friends.

Farringdon's home in the hollow bole of an oak, on a ferny mound. Dominic said that Nala (that was the dog's name) must have recalled what happened when Nobby Longtail Catt first arrived. Apparently, they set Nobby down in the middle of the carpet, just like they did with me years later, and Nala made a beeline for him. In a flash, Nobby squeezed under the settee out of reach and Nala, turning her head on one side, poked its muzzle under the settee. It jumped back with a yelp, having received a bunch of claws which left red lines across the nose.

Nobby must have been getting old or lazy, as there were mice living in the garden and one of them was foolhardy enough to venture into the house. Well, I soon made a meal of him and after that there were none of them to be seen in the garden either. Of course, the family knew me all along, as Nobby and I often went hunting together and played (and sometimes fought) in their back garden. I became Dominic's twin sister, Lisa's favourite, and inherited Nobby's cat bed. Farringdon called around to see my new home, and pronounced me the luckiest cat that ever lived, adding that I didn't deserve it, which was uncalled for, I thought. I suspected that now, as he was getting older, he was no longer quite so enamoured of his feral existence. After all, he wasn't born to such a life and had once lived a nice comfortable life in what was a nice comfortable house. My new home was very comfortable, I explored all the rooms and they were all super-except for the kitchen, which I hated. In a row along one wall were three large white boxes. With the one on the left, the whole front opened and Missus Jenkins put dirty dinner plates and things in it, shut the front and it made a funny noise for a long time. Later they would take out all the plates and things clean. The middle box had a round door in the middle of the front and they put dirty clothes in there. That made a funny noise too, rather longer than the one on the left and noisier too; in fact, for the last part it made a terrible noise. So much so, that I didn't really like going into the kitchen at all. The third box, the one on the right, looked just like the middle one but worked much more quietly. They took clean damp things out of the one in the middle and put them in the one on the right and later took them out again, quite dry. The trouble was that my bowl was in the kitchen so I just used to eat up my food as quickly as possible and get out of there as soon as I ever could.

Lisa was very kind to me but didn't understand that

I was a grown-up cat, not a kitten. She insisted on dangling a length of wool in front of me and expected me to chase it. Once, just to please her, I chased it for a moment or two, but I soon gave that up as it only encouraged her to expect me to do it all the time. Dominic was much more sensible. We used to explore the big back garden together and I showed him how one could find all sorts of interesting things hiding underneath the bushes or stones, like a fat juicy earthworm or even a hedgehog. I even took him into the forest and showed him Farringdon's home.

I visited Farringdon's home again a few days later. Going through the grassy field, I felt a few spots of rain and further into the forest it started raining heavily. I made my way through the masses of ferns that surrounded his home and popped straight through the hole, which was almost at ground level, inside and out of the rain.

"I see you've brought it with you, then!"

"Yes, I'm soaked. With all that rain, doesn't it just run down inside here?"

"No, I'm on the top of a little hill here—it all just runs away." And he was right, as the ferns stretched down the slope, away from the base of the oak tree, all the way round, down to one point where there was a deep cave running back into the hill. Under the weight of the rain the ferns were drooping their heads down, over the path to his door and that's how I got so wet.

"There's no point of us even thinking of going out at present, so let's just sit here and chat."

"What about?" grunted Farringdon and this was just the opening I needed.

"Well, for a start, you promised once to tell me how you got the name Farringdon Spanking Cat."

"All right then; my mum told me that her mum's mum said, the name Farringdon comes from an ancestor, years back, who came from that part of a town called London, wherever that is."

"I've never even heard of such a place. It can't be anywhere near here."

"Oh, it must be a long, long way away."

"Well, never mind that, how did you get the spanking bit? I hope you're not thinking of spanking me any day soon."

"You are an inquisitive cat, aren't you? Well then, just as it's still raining-whenever he was naughty, or what the big people thought was naughty, people where he lived spanked him on the rump-the obvious place to aim at. Since then, the first 'boy cat' in a cat's first litter has always been named Farringdon Spanking cat. Eventually, he ran away and lived on his own in a forest, just like me. Perhaps that's why it came so naturally to me."

Chapter 6
Back to the Big Lake

One day Farringdon and I were sunning ourselves just beside the big lake when he suddenly said, "This won't do, if we laze around like this; we're wasting our lives and we'll suddenly find we've got old. Think of somewhere, clever cat."

I thought a bit and then I had a brainwave, "We've only ever got half way round this lake; let's go and see the rest."

"You've only been half way around, that time when a man tried to drown two kittens. I've been right around, several times."

"All right then, clever whiskers, what's there to see?"

So, we set off, going the same way as before and, after several hours passed, the spot where we had rescued the two kittens. A long way after that there were houses alongside the road and as we went further there were more and more houses. I guessed that this is what they call a town. Then we came to a long, low building behind which were a string of long, low things like houses. Lots of the big people were going into them and then to my amazement the long, low houses moved off, one after the other and disappeared around a bend.

"There! What do you think of that? It's called a `train' and this place is called a `station'."

Lots of people think cats don't know any words, other than `pussy' or `tibs' or `din din' and this is perhaps true of a lot of pampered pets. But worldly-wise cats like Farringdon Spanking Catt keep their ears open and pick quite a few words. Just then another train arrived, coming from around the bend, stopped and lots of the big folk got out. I asked Farringdon where the people in the first train were going to and where the people in the second had come from.

"They were going to Buriton-on-sea and the others were coming from there. They were all coming home. This morning people came from there and others went to Buriton-on-sea."

"But that makes no sense; why don't the people from Buriton-on-sea just stay there and the people who went there stay at home? That way nobody need go anywhere."

"I hear what you say, but it's all to do with something called money."

"What's that?"

"It's what they need to get the lovely meaty food they give you out of the round tin box with a picture of a cat and squiggles on the front called writing. And, to get food for themselves of course and—oh, lots of other things; it's called 'buying' things. Mr Jenkins is old so he doesn't go anywhere by train any more, but he seems to get some money from somewhere. I just don't understand it."

"Well, if you don't, I'm sure I never will." And with that our conversation would have just petered out, but I wanted to know what was this 'sea' that Buriton was on.

"It's like the lake, only much bigger...much...much bigger. They say that if you go towards the rising sun or the setting sun or even crosswise to that, left or right, you will always eventually come to the sea. I just can't understand that."

But by now, it was starting to get dark and Farringdon said we had better be getting back. I remembered that it had taken us most of the day to get to the station, but we didn't go back the way we had come. Farringdon set off in the opposite direction and to my amazement we were back home before the light faded from the sky.

Chapter 7
Grandad Jenkins' Garden

Grandad Jenkins was very proud of his garden and grew all sorts of fruit and vegetables, so that the children's mum did not have to buy any, at least in summer and autumn. Even in winter he could dig up some pink roots called China rose, for use in a salad. But his real pride and joy were his tomatoes. I knew they should be red, because those were the ones mum brought home from the shops. But grandad's were yellow and as the crop was coming to an end, he would choose a nice big one, cut it open and spread out the pips on some fluffy stuff, he called blotting paper. When they were completely dry, he would collect them all up and put them into an envelope. He then did some of what they call writing on the front of the envelope and said to Dominic, "There, they'll give us a good crop next year of my prize sweet yellow tomatoes." I was quite proud to help him around the garden by keeping the mice away and stopping other cats scratching in the rows of peas, carrots or whatever to bury their business.

He sometimes complained about his knees-apart from digging, much of the sort of gardening he was so good at seemed to require him to be on his knees most of the time. Lisa's mum made up pads of several layers of old blanket all stitched together, with tapes top and bottom each side. With a pad on each knee, secured with the tapes behind each leg he could remain kneeling for hours. The garden was laid out in three parts; the nearest part to the house was about one hundred and fifty of my steps long, or about fifteen paces long in man size steps. It was all grassy and shaded by a lilac tree on one side and Dominic and Lisa's mum used to sit there on a chair that was never used indoors and lived in a shed all through the winter each year. Beyond that was another space, a bit larger than the first and here grandad grew lines of plants with green leaves and orange roots called, I think, carrots-and others consisting of nothing but pale green leaves and oh, lots of other things that Dominic said were all good to eat.

Beyond that again was a sort of shed all made of glass and things in there seemed to grow even in winter, or at least long before things outside. Beside it was a pile of grass cuttings, dead plants, leaves and things left over from cooking. Beyond that was a thick hedge and a line of trees marking the end of Grandad Jenkins' little world. I recognised most of the trees and could climb all of them except one that felt evil. I could not ever bear to climb it. Farringdon said it was called an ash tree and to me it somehow felt threatening.

I was very happy living with the Jenkins family; things felt very safe there and I could not imagine any crisis in the days, weeks and months ahead. Grandad worked in his garden when it wasn't raining; the twins Dominic and Lisa went to school in bursts of about five days followed by two at home. Farringdon told me that was called a week. I continued looking after all of grandad's plants and was proud of his skill in making them grow so strong and healthy. One day it grew very dark and by evening there was heavy rain. I was snug in my cat bed during that night when there were brilliant flashes of light followed by terrible loud noises, louder than ten times as loud as the loudest of the white boxes in the kitchen. I had seen and heard this before, although never quite so bad, so I just stayed curled up and waited for it to go away. But poor old Nala was a quivering mass of unhappy dog and Dominic stayed up with her, trying vainly to comfort her.

When it was over, we all tried to get some sleep, but there was a great noisy wind blowing for the rest of the night. The next day, Grandad Jenkins said he would have to go and see if the glasshouse was all right and if it was, pot up some cuttings he was raising. Mum said he should stay indoors, but he insisted and I went with him. The plants in the glass house were fine and grandad was soon busy when I started to get worried about a loud creaking noise. I scampered away as that evil ash tree fell, squashing the glass house and breaking all the glass. I dashed indoors and clawed at Dominic's ankles to make him follow me. He could see grandad all bent and squashed up and groaning. They sent for some men who arrived wearing helmets, in a large red lorry thing and they managed to prise the bent framework apart. They released grandad and a white vehicle took him away to a hospital. Mum, Dominic and Lisa all went too, but I stayed behind. I could smell the nasty mess where the trunk had broken in two just above ground level; it must have been like that and getting worse for ages. There was a big empty space now in the line of trees. The next day when Mum and the children went to the hospital to see how grandad was doing, they came back to the house afterwards with a man I had never seen before. Apparently, he was grandad's son, Mum's husband and the father of Dominic and Lisa.

I explained all this to Farringdon who said that just like us cats, some men did not stay around to see their litter grow up. After just another two visits, we never saw grandad's son again and after five weeks grandad came home from hospital. He could walk, but only with the aid of special walking sticks, called `crutches´ and he was always moaning about what needed doing in the garden. Dominic did his best to help but really had no idea how to go about it and I could see that his heart just wasn't in it; his hobby was everything `electrical´– electronics, he called it. Grandad gradually improved and after the rest of that summer and half the winter, he could busy himself in the garden again though heavy digging was out; he got a man in to do that.

Grandad Jenkins in his garden

Chapter 8
Our Great Adventure

Farringdon seemed extra lively that morning and instead of asking me to think of something to do, or complaining because I couldn't, he made a suggestion himself. I thought it the height of daring, or even foolhardy.

"Come on, then-you're going to enjoy this."

He set off around the lake, the opposite way from before and in no time, we arrived at the station. We slipped through the entry without anyone noticing us. We slipped onto a train and whenever anyone approached, we hid under a seat. Then it got busier and busier and we had to stay put.

"Isn't this a bit dangerous?"

"Not a bit, old boy, I've done it before, often, and always got back home safely, eventually."

Just then there was a jolt and the train started moving.

After what seemed an awful long time, the train stopped and all the big people got out. We waited until the coast was clear and then slipped out of the train and out of the station. I was very glad to get out as under the seat where we had been hiding it was dark, dirty, smelly and cramped. We slipped along the streets without attracting any attention, an art Farringdon had brought to perfection and which I had soon picked up. We soon came to a road which we crossed safely and then, beyond a pathway where people were sauntering along–they seemed to be on holiday–I saw it! I knew it could only be the magic lake you came to whichever way you went and realised that this must be the Buriton-on-Sea that Farringdon had told me about. What he hadn't said was that it smelt quite different from the lake at home. So, this was the sea and Farringdon said that all this sandy pebbly stuff was called a beach. We found the far end deserted so we were quite able to get right down to the water. I tasted the water and it was quite different from the stream near Farringdon's home, or the water Mum Jenkins put down for me. At first lick it was quite nice but when I tried some more, it soon became nasty. Farringdon said he had drunk too much once and it made him very ill. We explored the beach and the rest of the town and as the light began to fade, I said, "Surely, we had better see about going home. I hope you know how to do that."

"Oh, no problem, come on then."

But I was worried, Farringdon's assurance sounded a little vague. Still, we got onto what Farringdon said was the right train and settled down in the far end of a coach, out of sight. The train moved off and I was worried that the journey seemed to be taking much longer than coming; I could see Farringdon was looking worried too. We arrived at a station that didn't look anything like the one near our lake. I said that if this was the wrong place, we'd better get off now, or we would be even further from where we wanted to be. All of Farringdon's self-assurance had left him and he followed my lead as we jumped off. Outside the station, the road looked strange and we set off following our noses. We realised how long it was since we had eaten and how hungry we were. I led the way as I was sure I could smell fish and it led us to a yard behind a shop which sold all sorts of foods, including fish. The shop was busy with lots of the big people and we didn't dare enter, but around the back were untidy heaps of cabbage leaves, soft tomatoes and in a tin bucket there were fish heads; not cooked ones like I had enjoyed thanks to Missus in my first home, but we tucked in till we were full. We realised that hunger was the least of our problems—how on earth were we going to get back home? But if we were out of luck now, our luck was soon to get even worse. There were other feral cats living on the street just like us and some of them were really hostile. We found a corner to hide up in from where we could watch what was

The fallen tree crushed
Grandad's greenhouse,
with him trapped inside

going on, without being seen. Just at that moment, as two cats were having a fight, a white motor type thing with a picture of a cat on the side with some of that writing stuff, drew up and a big man got out. The cats were too busy fighting to notice him and he threw a net over them both, scooped them up, bundled them into the back of the motor and slammed the doors. Suddenly, all the other cats disappeared and as we explored the streets further, we noticed the van cruising around obviously looking for more cats to catch–though just why we had no idea; what were they going to do with all the cats they caught?

"I've half an idea what it's all about, but I wouldn't want to worry you with it."

"What do you mean?" I asked but he did not reply. The only thing to do was to make our way back to the station and get on a train we hoped would take us back to Buriton-on-Sea. As we neared the station, we were set upon by a gang of four cats and it might have gone badly for us but we were 'rescued' by further bad luck. The four cats disappeared as if by magic and a net was thrown over us. It only partly covered my body and I was able to wriggle free and disappear underneath a nearby car. Farringdon was not so lucky; he was bundled into the back of the cat catcher's van, which then drove off. Running as fast as ever my legs would take me, I kept the van in view until it turned left down a side road. As I reached the point where it had turned, I was just in time to see it turn right into a big yard surrounded by trees and bushes. I slipped in and made myself invisible among the bushes, from where I could see that the doors on the back of the van were open. I guessed Farringdon had been taken inside that big ugly brick building at the back of the yard. I stayed hidden until it got dark; there were lights on inside the big building. By the time it was really dark, people had left the building and driven away in cars, leaving the place deserted, though I could hear the cries of a number of cats, none of which I recognised. With the place now to myself, I set about exploring and on the side of the building found a window left ajar due to the hot weather. Jumping inside, I found rows and rows of cages, stacked four high, each with a cat inside; behind doors that looked like glass or something, at least one could see through them. I cried out 'Farringdon' and a voice answered 'over here'. He was in a cage on the lowest row but one and said that in fact, just like all the other cats, he had been provided with a bowl of really quite passable food, but that he'd swap the food for his freedom any day. He had seen a cat being taken out of a cage and another being put in one by a man turning a knob at the left-hand end of each door.

"See if you can get me out of here, there's a good chap."
"Right you are, if I can work the knob thing." But I had no idea how it worked. With my right forepaw I could just reach it with a stretch and tried pushing it to the left, then to the right, up or down, but it wouldn't budge and the door stayed shut. Pushing it in didn't work nor pulling it either, though that was difficult, needing two paws. The only thing left to try was turning it, but which way? And turning it with my paws didn't work, they just slipped, so I tried turning it with my mouth. This meant straining up even higher but with difficulty I got my jaws around it and tried turning it first this way and then that. It hurt my mouth and I could taste blood running down my throat but eventually with one last desperate effort, the door swung open. I don't know to this day whether it was turning it to the right or widdershins that worked but Farringdon hopped out and said 'thanks'.

We left that building in a hurry and made our way through the dark streets back to the station. When we had arrived, we had got off on the platform nearest the way out, so this time we went to the other platform. Some hours later, as it was getting light, a train arrived and we slipped in and hid under a seat. To our unimaginable relief, eventually we arrived at Buriton-on-Sea and held a plan-of-action conference. It was halfway through the morning and the station was very quiet-the morning rush hour was long over. So we decided we should wait until the late afternoon, when all those people who came to Buriton-on-Sea each morning were going home again, then we'd be sure to recognise some of them, take the same train as them and arrive back at the station near the lake. All went to plan, and as dusk approached, we were back at Farringdon's home in the base of the big oak. I said goodnight and less than an hour later, I popped through the cat flap in the door of the laundry room. A loud miaaaaaaaaou brought Lisa to me and she was delighted to see me, but scolded me for giving everyone a fright. I had to promise never to go away for two or three days together, ever again.

We relax on the sandy pebbly beach at Buriton-on-Sea

We arrived at a station
we didn't recognise

57

Chapter 9
A New Venture

To say that our great adventure had a profound effect upon me is a massive understatement but in the following days, I realised that it had had an even greater effect upon Farringdon. Never a frivolous cat like me, his demeanour was more subdued. He was realising that we were lucky to be free, to be alive, even; in particular that he was lucky to be alive, thanks to my valiant efforts to free him from the cage. Then, one day when I was exploring trees between the grassy field and Farringdon's oak home, I heard a plaintive miaow from down on the ground. Dropping down to see what was afoot, I found a young cat shivering with fright at being lost. I gave him a reassuring cuddle and asked what the problem was. It was the sort of story with which I was only too familiar, as indeed was Farringdon. Due to some change in domestic circumstances, this poor young cat, who said his name was Henry Wellington Green Catt, had found himself homeless. Catt is a courtesy title or surname to which every cat is entitled though many often don't bother.

I told him to follow me and led him to the oak on the ferny down.

"Hello, what have you there?"

"This is Henry Wellington Green Catt and the poor lad has been booted out of his home. We will have to try and sort out his problem."

"Funny you should bring up this sort of thing just now. Ever since our not-so-great adventure, I've been thinking that instead of just amusing ourselves and wasting our lives, we ought to be doing something for the feline world as a whole."

"What exactly have you in mind?" Farringdon reminded me that when I was booted out of my first home, Tommy had found a new home for me.

"We should set up an organisation to place displaced cats in new homes."

And that is how the Feline Society for the Assistance of Homeless Cats was founded. I said Farringdon should be the president and chairman and he said I should take on the role of secretary. I co-opted William Choco Brown Catt to join the committee as membership secretary with special responsibility for recruitment. The very first success of the Feline Society for the Assistance of Homeless Cats was with the placement of Henry with a rich widowed lady called Rosa, who could never bear to turn away a cat in need, and Henry joined the other nineteen cats in her home. That we happened to know that new placement was a possibility, was a lucky fluke, we could not reasonably expect the good lady to accept another cat every time a new emergency arose. So the committee members of the Feline Society for the Assistance of Homeless Cats–Farringdon, William and myself–vowed to set up a network of correspondents to notify when a new placement became available and/or when an unfortunate cat found him or herself homeless, so that we could match up one with the other. William Choco Brown set about creating the network with commendable energy and enthusiasm. He was fortunate that Rosa, in whose home he lived, was very easy-going about his tendency to disappear for a day or two, or even three in a row. He used this time to spy out the ground for miles around his home and get to know the local cat population. South, east and west he recruited a local cat to be a deputy membership secretary, thus covering a wide area.

Cats were eager to offer their service. The idea was that each deputy membership secretary should recruit from his part of the area, several assistant deputy membership secretaries; all cats just love an important sounding title. This way, any available placement or homeless cat in need of one would be reported up through the chain of command, so that the one could be matched up with the other. At the next formal committee meeting, only three weeks after setting up the scheme, William Choco Brown was proudly able to report that deputy membership secretaries had been appointed south, east and west and each of these had at least one assistant deputy membership secretary. Thus, all told the Feline Society for the Assistance of Homeless Cats now had thirteen active members and William hoped shortly to appoint a deputy and at least two assistant deputies in the northern region. At the next committee meeting, it was announced that the Society now had in all twenty-five active members and that seven homeless cats had found placements. A target of one hundred active members by the end of the year was proposed and adopted.

Chapter 10
Epilogue

I am now a very old cat, a very very old cat but my memory is as good as ever and I love reminiscing about all the interesting, strange and remarkable things I have experienced. My friend Farringdon and I have had some wonderful, funny, unforgettable and even frightening experiences too, but oh dear, that was all so many summers ago. Alas Farringdon is no longer with us; he was quite a few years older than me and, musing upon what little time he had left to live, he explained that as the end drew near, he would clean and tidy up his home in the bole of the oak tree situated on the summit of the ferny down and leave it ready for its next occupant, while he went away and found somewhere quiet to curl up and enter the long sleep. He must have done just that—there was always the disused old badger set or rabbit warren around—for on my last visit to his home it was abandoned, clean and tidy just as he had promised. But I am sure that he was proud of what we had achieved; him, William Choco Brown and I, and others coming after us. For the Feline Society for the Assistance of Homeless Cats continues to flourish, being now in the hands of new committee members, and the total membership, including all the deputy membership, and assistant deputy membership secretaries, now comfortably exceeds one hundred. William Choco Brown's successor tells me that since it was founded, the Society has rehomed no less than two hundred and fifty needy cats. In memory of Farringdon Spanking Catt, his oak tree home is now maintained as temporary stop-gap accommodation for any hapless cat while 'we', the Society, arrange a new placement. I believe that the big people have a similar arrangement for any of their youngsters in need, which is a nice thought.

Here, in the Jenkins household where I still live, there have been big changes. Mrs Jenkins, Dominic and Lisa's mother slipped quietly away last winter, and to my surprise and disgust, her husband–Grandad Jenkins's son–did not even attend the wake. On a happier note, Grandad Jenkins is still around although nowadays, he only ventures out into his beloved garden on warm dry days. The twins are now grown up, Lisa has a husband and Grandad Jenkins is looking forward to his first great grandchild. So all in all, I have nothing to complain about and just take every day as it comes; indeed, as Farringdon once told me, I am the luckiest cat alive.

Addendum

Yellow Laughing S. Catt never did tell Farringdon Spanking Catt what the S. stood for, as he was too embarrassed. On account of his rather short legs, other cats scoffed at him, calling him sausage cat on account of a fancied similarity to a Dachshund or `sausage dog`.

Page 37 Originally a small hamlet, Farringdon is now a part of Islington. The name signifies a fern covered hill or `ferny down`.

Page 34 Nala was a Belgian shepherd dog. In Swahili, Nala means `a gift` and she came to the Jenkins family when they adopted her to save her from being put down; the dog charity in question being simply overwhelmed by stray dogs.

Page 42 Winter radishes, the popular variety China rose, provides radishes when other varieties are out of season.